WHO AM I

THE TRILOGY

HANIFA IHECHI

Order this book online at www.trafford.com
or email orders@trafford.com

Most Trafford titles are also available at major online book retailers.

Note for Librarians: A cataloguing record for this book is available from Library
and Archives Canada at www.collectionscanada.ca/amicus/index-e.html

Printed in Victoria, BC, Canada.

ISBN: 978-1-4269-0772-2 (sc)

*We at Trafford believe that it is the responsibility of us all, as both individuals
and corporations, to make choices that are environmentally and socially sound.
You, in turn, are supporting this responsible conduct each time you purchase a
Trafford book, or make use of our publishing services. To find out how you are
helping, please visit www.trafford.com/responsiblepublishing.html*

*Our mission is to efficiently provide the world's finest, most comprehensive
book publishing service, enabling every author to experience success.
To find out how to publish your book, your way, and have it available
worldwide, visit us online at www.trafford.com*

Trafford rev. 7/2/2009

www.trafford.com

North America & international
toll-free: 1 888 232 4444 (USA & Canada)
phone: 250 383 6864 ♦ fax: 250 383 6804
email: info@trafford.com

TABLE OF CONTENTS

WHO AM I

Who am I
That you should be mindful of
This is the question King David asked
Today I ask the same
CREATOR, who am I
Are you not yet ashamed
Why should you feel proud of me
Why do you bless me
With feelings of security
Here comes Armageddon
The greatest of all wars
I behold your angels
Risking their lives for me

Who am I
That you should be mindful of
I no longer abide by your law
I have created my own society
I make the rules, I control my destiny
I reign using power, might, and destruction
Everyone obeys my instructions
If they don't I will rain down chaos and tribulations
Do you believe you're in control, FATHER
Hell no, I am

Who am I
That you should be mindful of
You create universes
I build atomic and nuclear bombs
I am a murderer without a conscience
All wicked things become my intention
Look at me, I rule this land
But why question me

Was that not your original plan
I position satellites into space
So I can spy on everyone's domain
The path I follow is dark and cold
You know as I do FATHER
I have lost my soul
I distastefully boast about my disgrace
Should you question me
I will shove it in your face

Who am I
That you should be mindful of
I am the burden to human love
I promote hunger and disease
By the stroke of a pen I can make it cease
Why should I promote peace
When living as a leech is what I believe
Who cares about those getting hurt
When my bank account is about to burst
Please, do not call upon your faithful followers
History will prove that they can be much worst

CREATOR, who am I
That you should be mindful of
Behold, the seed of your greatest creation

Seed

I will plant a seed today
I will love and nurture it
It will grow strong and wild
Occupying acres of land

Its vines will know no boundaries
The community, the nation
Indeed the world
Shall flock to my land

Kings and queens, pharaohs and czars
Shall bow their knees
When they behold your might
Your power, your majesty
You will eliminate all the competition
Here comes the ones who answers my call

And does my bidding
I see them gathered at my gate
Digging for scraps in my garbage
Oohh the terrible fate that awaits them

My tree and I will conquer all
We will rule the air and land
We will control food and water
We will rule the world
I will rule like a god
I – will – be – goooddd

Today, I will plant a seed
But unbeknown to me
My neighbor had already planted a seed
And it is already growing

THE SCAVENGERS ARE HERE

The scavengers are here
Gathering for the feast
They can be seen in the air
Encircling their prey
They unleash destruction
Bomb, bomb away
Obliterating everything.
Where once stood a building

A castle you may call it
Tall and majestic
It's the pride of its people
Now in its stead
It cannot be believed
The voidless form of a shell
A creator in its place
The scavengers are here

They will fall on their prey
Plucking first the eyes
So their scavenger ways
Will not be realized
They will then rip the throat
So the prey cannot shout
Next the belly will tear open
To expose all the bowels
While the prey lay there kicking

So lock up your doors
Abandon your way of life
Run to the hills and hide
For they will not tire
In their destructive manner
And they will not leave
Until the town is bare
All hopes are abandoned
Because the scavengers are here.

Innocence Forgotten

A child came into the world
She walked in the land of fairies and princesses
A land where knights battle the dragons
To rescue the fair damsel
Where good conquers evil
Where the gods favor the humans
A land where magic is real
And mythical creatures exist

But alas, the child will be forced into another world
Where good does not always win
Where right and wrong are not easily deciphered
Where the strong makes life
Unbearable for the weak
The child tries in vain to hold on to the fantasy
But like a mirage, it kept floating away
Farther and farther away until nothing

The child grows up to give birth to innocence
As she falls in love with her bundle of joy
She knows her innocence will one day
Grow up into a land of fairies and knights
But a sad thought crossed her mind
As she knows the fantasy will not last
For innocence will meet the world
And one by one the stories will fade away
As the world chisels them all away.

MOTHER EARTH

Mother earth was angry
Get up, how can you sleep
A great wrong has been done to me
I ran to the hills where I looked down
All around were burning towns
I ran for days as I lost count
Of dismembered bodies strewn around

There in the distance
Far, far away
An army so mighty
You tremble with fear
I ran to the commander
To ask what happened here
No need to worry

Pick up a weapon
Come join our army
We have rid the earth
Of the evil within
Infiltrate and dominate everything
On whose orders you did these things
On the highest one there is

Our god commanded these things
God would command genocide
Over one million dead
This is not divine it is a crime
Sir, I know not of your god or whence he came
But I do know my god and yours
Cannot be one and the same

ABOMINABLE LIE

From the simmering rubbles you rose
From the ash of war you were formed
Over all the nations you tower
You are the abominable lie
You have failed in your every task
You did not stop the Rwanda genocide
You did not stop the Yugoslavia massacre
You have not stopped any war

By being brave in Sudan
You hope to cover your shame of Iraq
You enforce your regulations on weaker nations
But monitor not the greater
The bold one ignores you
While the follower laughs
You are their puppet on a string
The world's greatest laughing thing

What will become of you
Oh mighty disgusting one
When the eyes of the world has opened
And it is realized you are nothing
But an abominable lie

I Cannot Believe

I can believe the moon is not round
The sun is not the center of our solar system
The sky is not blue but black
There is no bottom to the ocean

I believe I can walk on water
Soar above the heavens
Command the forces of nature
Cheat death if I have to

I can believe in the existence of a god
With a mind so powerful HE create universes
My faith in HIM is solid, unshaken, immovable, deeply rooted
Though I have never seen HIM

Still, it is your words that knock me off my foundation
Of all the things I believe in
I cannot believe you do not love me.

I DO NOT UNDERSTAND

I heard a loud explosion
It sounded like ten thunders
I heard another
Then I heard another again
I ran from my bed
I don't know where to hide
Please somebody tell me
I do not understand

I heard the people running
I could hear the children scream
My father ran to help
My mother hugged me
We stayed in my room
Where we waited all night
Why won't my father return
I do not understand

I looked through my window
The night had turned to day
The sky was so bright
The fear almost went away
But then I went deaf
And the house started to shake
For on the ground where I live
Was a strong fear of death

I looked to my mom
Where is my dad
She tried to hug and comfort me
But I ran into the street
For I just had to see
Imagine my shock, my disbelief
The man that I love
Shot down in the street

Someone come please
Sit down and tell me
I do not understand
Explain it to me
Like a dog my father
Is shot down in the street
Please explain it to me
I do not understand

DEATH IS HERE

I jumped up in bed
From the loud bang overhead
I looked through my window
The sky became as morning
And then I heard the screaming
I knelt in the bed
Fear gripped my legs
As the house kept on shaking
From the force of the bombing
I saw mama calling
I cannot hear her words
For the noise is so deafening
I did not feel when he lifted me
I knew only I was moving
I looked up in my father's face
And realized that he carried me
Only then did I see
My clothes had turn to red
A shrapnel protruded from my head
Though I felt no pain
Yet the cold gripped me in a tight embrace and I knew immediately
Death is here

I Saw Something Today

I saw something today
It held my gaze
I could not break that stare
I was rooted there in place
It flooded me like a tidal wave
Drowning me in memories
Of sitting on the veranda
In the dead of night
Listening to the thunderous
Crash of the waves
Enjoying the warm sea air
I saw something today

It was mesmerizing, tantalizing,
Stimulizing, hypnotizing
It brought a smile to my lips
Made my heart wanna sing
It brought out a longing
That did not exist
Today I saw it again
Now I know what's amiss
I felt joy, laughter, happiness
Hallelujah, hallelujah
I saw something today
As I walked across
The Rose Hill lawn
And looked up on
A clear sky in May
I saw a full moon today

MOTHERS DEATH

Who is responsible for my mothers' death
On whose shoulder should the blame lie
Whose head will be demanded in revenge
I don't care about your stupid war
I don't care about your chivalry
I don't want your grief or sorrow
I just need my mother
To hug and comfort me

Daddy stood there shaking
He hasn't been the same
I know this will prove risky
Yet as I opened the coffin
I saw the shock, there was no awe
As the guests tried to comprehend
The bullet riddled charred remains
Of what was once my best friend

That night as I knelt to pray
I cried to my creator to seek my revenge
Rain down her blood upon their heads
Uproot and leave them childless
Come now father tuck me in bed
Tell me in the morning
All will have been a bad dream
For this I know they will have us believe

AMERICAN SOLDIER

I am a defender of freedom
Not the destroyer of it
I am the protector of democracy
Not an enforcer of it
I am a savior to the innocent
Not their persecutor
I am the muscle of the weak
Not their judge

I am an American Soldier
I fight to protect the Constitution
Do not destroy it
I am the shield of America
No one will invade
Do not make unnecessary enemies
I am the sword of America
I strike with precision
Do not create animosity
I am the spine of America
On my shoulders rest her sovereignty
Do not jeopardize it

You are my leaders
From you I seek guidance
Do not lead me astray
Do not deceive me
Do not lead me to shed innocent blood
This will haunt me
I will be despised by all nations
And become the conscience of our people

Let HONOR be your beacon
Clothe yourself in INTEGRETY
Never lose focus of DUTY
SELFLESS SERVICE keeps you humble
Let your LOYALTY fuel your PERSONAL COURAGE
RESPECT life and God will RESPECT you
Live by these codes which guides us
This will keep America proud

I Have Loved You

How much do I love you
The words do not exist
For I have loved you before the blissful day we met
Before I entered my mothers' womb
Before the beginning of time
I have loved you
Before the universe came into being
Before the angels were created
I have loved you
From God wrote my name next to yours
I have loved you
With every organ in this body
Every strand of hair, every drop of blood
I have loved you
With my most inner being, the hidden part of me
The spirit that exist in me
How much do I love you
Can you measure the beginning of time
My love is a thousand times more
And after this life
In infinity shall we be united forevermore

WHO AM I

Who am I
That you should be mindful of
This same question King David asked
Today I pose it again
Creator, who am I
What am I

When I stood in the midst of emptiness
And I beheld your magnificence
The suns and the planets
The entire solar systems
They exist to the farthest reach of space
Then what am I
That you cease to let me be extinct

Of what use am I to my own state of being
What contribution can I make
To the earth's galaxy
As I stare at the Milky Way
I know I am not needed here
Have I not failed in every task given me

I have killed my neighbors
Tortured the animals
Eradicate the trees
My own madness drives me
To conquer the galaxy
Is there to be no limit to my stupidity
Why do you cease to let me be extinct
When I stood before your entire creation
The earth was but a speck of sand
Then where do I fit in your master plan

For out of love
You created me to stand in awe of these things
Out of love
You commanded the animals to fear me
Out of love
I am to care for all living things

Is my existence worth this
What contribution have I made to anything
From the morning when I rise
To the evening when I sleep
My thoughts are filled with wickedness
I think only of ways to exploit
And satisfy my crave
I am a cancer in the land
Then why do you cease to let me be extinct
Who am I
Oh Glorious One
That you should be mindful of

IN MEMORIAL

I wish I could say how I truly feel
But such words have never been spoken
I wish I could express my feelings
But such words have never been written
No one can comprehend the depth of our friendship
And no one ever will

You are my friend
Has always been my friend
Will always be my friend
Death will not part us forever
It has succeeded in this lifetime
It will fail in the next
How do I honor our friendship

Can anyone honor the dead
But I wish I were there
To cradle and protect you from harm
I wish I were there
Like the Eiffel tower by your side
I wish I were there to die
But I survived

And because I do you will be remembered
I will spend my life bringing to justice
Those who did injustice to you
I will call upon the GOD of my Mothers
For he is a great lover of justice
He will expose them
And bring them to great shame and ruin

I will then build you a memorial
That you may never be forgotten
SOLDIER
I salute you
I salute you
I salute you
Thank you and goodbye my friend

THEY ARE NOT OF US

We are a people
With a history so grand
Through many a centuries
And evolving we have come
We have had our differences
And settled them with war
In our infancy we have grown
We have all come so far

We have stood together
In times of great trouble
We band to rid ourselves
The tyrants we have nurtured
Now there is a group
Who does not share in our adventures
Their personal agenda
Is not to improve us

Throughout the ages of time
They have lived among us
They have slithered along
Like the snakes of Moses
Hiding like shadows on walls
They have remained non-existent
Making changes in our lives
They are not of us

How I Love You

From the first time our eyes locked
We became one
From the first time we touched
We became inseparable
From the first time we kissed
We experienced bliss
From the first time we embraced
We knew we were blessed

I don't know why but when I think of you
I get this funny feeling in my tummy
When you lay there sleeping
I become so overwhelmed
Just watching you that, yes
Sometimes I breakdown and cry

I now understand that
I don't need to climb mountains
I don't need to swim across oceans
I don't need to brave the elements

Love is not to be conquered
It is not to go in search of
Love already exists within me
You however are the match
That ignites the flame in me
And now love clearly sees

How much do I love you
The words do not exist
For I am a lioness
Yet I am humbled
I am a rock
Yet I melt
I am a dagger
But it is my heart being pierced

I cannot tell the future
Neither will I try
But for this very moment
I will honor you
For this very minute
I will love you
For this very second
I will praise you

Tomorrow will honor itself
But for today
To honor, love and praise you
Is the only way I know to say
How much I truly love you

PUPPET ON A STRING

I am a puppet on a string
I possess no will
They have clipped my wings
Now they control the strings

Oh the wealthy they do cheer me
While the peasants they do hate me
They have pelted me with rotten eggs
And jeered at me with clenched fists
If they stop to really look at me
They would understand my plight you see
For of my own I have no will
I am simply a puppet on a string

They have paved the road for prophecy
To happen here and now
They have set the stage and made me play my role
I have been appointed star of the show
Now the audience is filled with glee
But I am not what I appear to be
I am only a puppet on a string

I am a puppet on a string
I possess no will
They have clipped my wings
Now they control the strings

THE SPIRIT OF MANKIND

When the British government
Oppressed the citizens of America
The people defied them
When the British troops
Marched against the people
The people defied them
When it seem the British would win
And independence was lost
The people continued to defy them
This is not only an American spirit
This is the spirit of mankind

When the Africans were kidnapped
And taken by the slave traders
The Africans defied them
When they were sold as cargo
And separated from their families
The Africans defied them
Faced with degradation, whipping
Loss of limb and life
Still the Africans continued to defy
For such is the spirit of mankind

When the French people rejected
The hypocrisy of the French bureaucracy
The people defied them
When the French troops marched in
To put down the rebellion
The people defied them
Faced with the prospect of
The plague, starvation and a grim future
The people continued to defy them
For this is the spirit of mankind

When you march against
Your own citizens
The people will defy you
When you impose your will
On the world
The world will defy you
Faced with your superior weapons
Of mass destruction and annihilation
The world will unite in defiance
For this is mankind's
God given right to life
This is the spirit of mankind

ALL DAY LONG

I sat there watching you labor
All day long
You do not take breaks
Neither do you stray
All you do is labor
All day long

Do you know your commander
Who stands guard over you
Do you know the queen
For whom you labor earnestly
Do you know the reason
You will survive us through the ages

You are a master architect
Yet you see not these things
A colony you create
Still you see none of these
Warehouses full of tasty things
And still you take no pride in these

You wonderful beast of burden
Carrying eight times your weight
Yet not once did rebellion
Ever cross your trait
I do wish every human
Was as disciplined as an ant

WONDEROUS JOY

You gently touch my cheek
While I lay there asleep
You fill me with wondrous joy
Truly you are unique

A blanket you become
To shelter me from winter
A soothing calming air
To cool me in the summer

You are my survival
I am filled with hope and peace
You are my wondrous joy
My fresh gentle breeze

The Prophet Came Today

The prophet came today.
Tired, hungry and dusty yet did not stop to rest.
At the rising of the sun the prophesying began.
From the middle of the street the prophet pleaded
"Repent, repent, repent, for the wrath of the hand of God is near."
The people snickered and asked
"From whence did you come?"
"Old and ragged I AM, my appearance unkempt
My clothes ravaged from the distance of time
I have come from the beginning of the Euphrates
I have traveled the hills of Kedar
I have lived on the mount of Zion
Should I become a stranger in this land?
For seven years she has been given grace
For seven years she sinned a little more
Six messengers came before, after me there will be no more.
Now the Deliverer is close at hand."

The people shouted with glee
"Yes, let the Deliverer come and deliver us from this wicked world."
The prophet replied
"The Deliverer is here to deliver the wrath of God."
The people were highly incensed at what the prophet said
"Know you not that we are the people of God
Know not that God has blessed us in all our endeavors,
So much that we have become the greatest nation
Why now would He seek to destroy our mighty city?"
"O children of the lie
You have deceived the whole world into thinking you are a great
    nation
When in fact you are a great magician.
You are a master of light and glass
By the two devices you have deceived the majority

But where would you be without your bag of tricks
So much have you told the lie, you actually believe it.
But the Deliverer is close at hand, repent I say
No mercy will be shown, young and old, great and small
The foundation of the nation will be shaken and the city will
    be no more.
She will stand a relic of the city that was"
Consumed by anger the people grabbed the prophet
They beat, kicked and threw the prophet in jail
Yet the prophet continued to wail.
"Repent, repent, repent, for the hand of the wrath of God is near."

The next day the people pleaded with the prophet to leave
"We have had no rest because of you constant wailing.
Here is food, water, and horse, now go and do not return."
"I cannot leave until I am sure you have heard the message
You have plugged you ears, loudly played your music
But you have not listened."
At hearing this, the people whispered among themselves
"What if it is all true? What if a deliverer is coming?
We should do what our fathers before us did
We will coerce the powerful nations to be our allies.
We will use the prophet.
Surely with the prophet here the Deliverer will not enter the city
When any misfortune that should befall a nation
We will accuse that nation of being ungodly.
We will tell them the Deliverer had entered their city
Then rent them the prophet to send away the Deliver.
At this point, we will charge an exorbitant amount of money
When the money is no more, we will demand their land.
This we will do until we own all the nations.
Yes, it is all clear now; do you not see fellow citizens?
God indeed sent us the prophet that these things may be fulfilled
Truly God is with us."

As the people reveled in their newly formed plan
They bound the prophet to the walls of the temple
And amidst the noise of the celebration was the faint wailing of the
    prophet
"Repent, repent, repent, for the hand of the wrath of God is near."
At the stroke of midnight an uneasy chill filled the air
The sleeping became restless, the celebration stopped
All eyes lifted to the temple, the wailing had ceased.
The bereaved prophet looked at the city with tearful eyes and a sor-
    rowful heart
And prophesied in that mighty city one last time,
"Doom has come your way. The Deliverer is here."

On my way to work this morning
The police were arresting an individual for obstructing traffic and
    disturbing the peace.
As I drove by I heard the never ending wailing of a cry
"Repent, repent, repent, for the hand of the wrath of God is near."
The prophet came today.

WHO AM I

Who am I
I pray this may be the last time
That I will have to ponder this question
As I meditate upon the answer
Inspiration came from the Creator
First I existed in His mind
From His thoughts I moved to the drawing board
He became infatuated with the idea
He would create a being called human

At first He created all the animals
But they lacked the spirit of development
HE then envisioned ha-adam
He had created the perfect human
He taught the nature of everything to Adam
And encouraged its progression
With His hands He built a home for Adam
With his DNA He fashioned an Eve

The Creator had a great vision
Of a world in harmony with humans
They would populate the earth
Until they begin to explore the universe
I was passed down from the loins of Adam
Through the womb of Eve I came to be
I am the will of the Creator
I am that which He had envisioned

Give me the courage of David
Make me as brave as Deborah
Bless me with the meekness of Moses
Make me as faithful as Job
Grant me the wisdom of Solomon

Bless me with the knowledge of Adam
Set me on fire like Caiaphas
Bless me with the blessings of Yeshua
Shower me with all of your blessings
Clothe me with you love and mercies

Mother Eve gave birth to humanity
From her breast we drank the milk of life
For any man to disrespect a woman
Is to bring shame to the wife of Adam
For a man to hate and despise her
Is to hate the creation of God
No one was born to live in misery
No one was born to live in fear

Do not treat me disrespectfully
Do not place in me inferiority
Throw off the chains of destruction
Free your mind from the shackles of conflict
Let us work to abolish poverty
Let us work to live in peace and unity
This is the will of the Almighty
A world in harmony with humans

Let us walk through the hills of El Shaddi
Let us offer praises unto Yahweh
Let us prostrate ourselves before Allah
Let us call upon the guidance of Jehovah

Who am I
I know this is the last time
That I will ever need to ponder this question
I was just a fantasy, a thought
I dwelled in the greatest mind of all
In His image I was fashioned
To be created with all HIS qualities
And now I know with all certainty
I am a child of the Almighty

The Matriarch

I woke this morning to the terrible reminder
The matriarch is gone
Grief and anger filled my most inner being
My soul is being tortured
Grief continues its never ending stabbing
Piercing the very heart
Cutting the link between body and soul

Midnight again
I shall stay awake until morning light
Tossing and turning, waking and sleeping
Torturous grief will you never lead me to peace

Serenity has fled from me
My brain no longer seeks rest
I opened my mouth to scream but words took flight from me
Rigor took hold of me
Why has death forsaken me

In sheer shock I must perform the tasks of the day
Living without a reason, existing without a cause
The very heart of my being has being ripped out of me
Why does the world not cease to exist
To face the world without a care
Is too great a burden to bare

Evening again, torturing time,
I lay on my bed of thorns
My eyelids close, another dreamless night
No visions of her forms in my head
Three hours or four, I will not have five
That is the rest allotted me
In the morning I woke to the terrible reminder
The matriarch is gone

MOTHER

You are taller than the highest mountain
The pillow on which I rest my head
Yours are the arms that shielded me
From all of life's infirmities
The womb that cradled me
Until you gave birth to me

You are worth
More than the finest crystals
More than silver and gold
More than the diamonds of Africa
Way more than Solomon's treasures

You have earned the right
You have worked for the title
And now I crown you
MOTHER!!!!!!!

MY CHILD

I woke to teeny tiny hands
Exploring my face
I opened my eyes to
The greatest gift God granted me
My child
A smile formed across my lips
As I stared into those
Big beautiful innocent eyes
I am greeted also with a smile

Driven by curiosity
The hands continue their never-ending adventure
Tugging at the nose and ear
Wondering about the texture and colour
Poking at the eyes with great interest
These have a glossy sheen
Touching those milky teeth
These are completely different

Overcome by a mother's instinctive love and joy
I lifted her to the heavens and once more gave God thanks
For my bundle of joy
My love, my pride, my all
My child

My Rose

My rose is like a gift to me
Sweet smelling, soft and beautiful
It caresses me with tenderness
I take delight in pleasing it

My rose is like sweet memories
Pleasing to the soul
It brings a smile across my lips
In days of my darkest hour

My rose is like a lioness
Knowing honor, courage and loyalty
It grows only in my garden
And blooms for none other

My rose knows its gardener
Each petal is known by me
I will love, honor, and cherish this rose
My rose is like a gift to me

TO THE CREATOR'S DELIGHT

Oh say can you see, in the dawn's morning light
A land of hills and valleys
Of plains basking in the sunlight.
A melting pot of colours, a mixture of God's grace
I see the shade of promise
Of yellow, brown, dark and pale
I see God's spirit glowing
It encircles in the air

I see a land that's buzzing with cultures so divine
I salute you brave warrior
Keeper of the land
A handsome in his kilt hugging tightly his bagpipe
The Russians have invaded
Oh what a joyous sight
It's that time again Kwanza is in the air
Ramadan must cleanse us of our sins and
Hanukkah burned in our brain
West Indian day parade captures my heart each year
It's the taming of a day
When our pride we lay bare
But what is this
Something old is again new
For this land has now embraced the mighty Spanish tongue

Oh say can you see, in the dawn's morning light
A land beaming with every culture
To the Creator's delight
There is no division in country, race or in creed
In the Creator's eyes
America is one country

THERE IS

There is no religion
There is only one Supreme Being
There is no earth
There is only the universe
There is no different culture
There is only the human race
There is no black or white
There is only day and night
There is no rich and poor
There is only need for more
There is no sickness and death
There is only life and health
There is no injustice
There is only your conscience
There is no young or old
There is only what you have known
There is no right or wrong
There is only the law of love
There is no country or border
There is only land and water
There is no politics or oppression
There is only mental emancipation
There is no high or low
There is only one way to go
There is no strong or weak
There is only the strength you can will
There is no shackling of feet
There is only the freedom you give
There is no big or small
There is only one size fits all
There is no you or I
There is only the great I AM
There is no he or she
There is only the way it should be

LIFE

What is life
Is it a dream of is it reality
Is it a mirage, an illusion
A figment of our imagination
Is this life truly happening
Do you hear the words I speak
Or do you imagine it
Is this body really me
Or a representation of what I am
When I touch you
How can you tell if I'm being friendly
When thousands of nerves react in an instant
Sending messages to the brain
That interprets the reaction as friendly
All within a nanosecond
When miracles like these happen
Do you believe I can tell you what life is

So then, to what can life be compared
It is the passion in the midst of a couple's lovemaking
It is the orgasm
It is the banding of wind and rain
That cuts a path of death and destruction
It is the eye of the hurricane
It is that which holds the earth together
When she trembles and rips herself apart
It is the lava in the volcano

LIFE
Is the first cry of a newborn
It is the wisdom in the advice of the elders
It is the laughter of the hyena
And the roar of a lion

LIFE
Is men dying for their faith
Women fighting for equality
A people massing together in unity

LIFE
Came out of the French revolution
The toppling of Nazi Germany
The struggle in the war against apartheid

LIFE
Is never ending
Always producing
Regenerating
Reincarnating
Always existing
Never condescending
Degenerating
Disintegrating
Never retreating
Always creating
Forever forthcoming
Always superior
Always prodigious
Never patronizing
Never inferior
LIFE
Is the force which flows
From the womb of the Creator
And comes into existence

LIFE
Is the Word which was spoken and now Is
And since life comes from the Creator
Who is the essence of love
Then to live life
Is to be loved
Because life
Life is love

A THOUGHT

A thought
Came into being
The thought gained consciousness
The consciousness manifested a body
The body developed emotions
The thought is
I AM